Magic Puppy

Magic Puppy

Star of the Show

SUE BENTLEY

Illustrated by Angela Swan

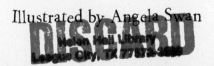

GROSSET & DUNLAP
Published by the Penguin Group
Penguin Group (USA) Inc., 375 Hudson Street, New York, New York 10014, USA
Penguin Group (Canada), 90 Eglinton Avenue East, Suite 700,
Toronto, Ontario M4P 2Y3, Canada
(a division of Pearson Penguin Canada Inc.)
Penguin Books Ltd., 80 Strand, London WC2R 0RL, England
Penguin Group Ireland, 25 St. Stephen's Green, Dublin 2, Ireland
(a division of Penguin Books Ltd.)
Penguin Group (Australia), 250 Camberwell Road, Camberwell, Victoria 3124, Australia
(a division of Pearson Australia Group Pty. Ltd.)
Penguin Books India Pvt. Ltd., 11 Community Centre, Panchsheel Park,
New Delhi—110 017, India
Penguin Group (NZ), 67 Apollo Drive, Rosedale, North Shore 0632, New Zealand
(a division of Pearson New Zealand Ltd.)
Penguin Books (South Africa) (Pty.) Ltd., 24 Sturdee Avenue,
Rosebank, Johannesburg 2196, South Africa

Penguin Books Ltd., Registered Offices:
80 Strand, London WC2R 0RL, England

Text copyright © 2008 Sue Bentley. Illustrations copyright © 2008 Angela Swan. Cover
illustration copyright © 2008 Andrew Farley. First printed in Great Britain in 2008 by
Penguin Books Ltd. First published in the United States in 2009 by Grosset & Dunlap, a
division of Penguin Young Readers Group, 345 Hudson Street, New York, New York 10014.
GROSSET & DUNLAP is a trademark of Penguin Group (USA) Inc. Printed in the U.S.A.

Library of Congress Cataloging-in-Publication Data is available.

ISBN 978-0-448-45047-6   10 9 8 7 6 5

To Butch—a boisterous playmate
with a mind of his own.

Prologue

Storm, the young silver-gray wolf froze as a terrifying howl rose into the air.

"Shadow!" Storm gasped. The big, fierce lone wolf, who had attacked Storm's wolf pack and left his mother wounded, was very close.

Storm had to act fast. He decided to use his magic. Suddenly a dazzling flash of bright golden light and a shower of sparks filled the air. Where the young wolf had stood there now crouched a tiny rusty-colored spaniel puppy with wavy fur, long floppy ears, and midnight-blue eyes.

Storm's puppy heart beat fast as he bounded forward across the snow. He looked from left to right, trying to find a hiding place, but the flat plain stretched in all directions like a white desert.

He saw a tiny speck in the distance, which was growing bigger as it came closer. It was an adult wolf.

Storm whimpered with terror.

His wobbly legs collapsed beneath him and Storm felt himself sinking. Chunks of snow rained onto the little puppy as he sank down into an ice cave. He lay there trembling, hoping that his hiding place would protect him.

Moments later, Storm heard paws

scraping above him as a large animal stood in the entrance to the cave. This was it.

A wolf's head appeared, framed by the night sky. "Are you hurt, my son?" growled a soft velvety voice.

"Mother!" Storm woofed in relief, wagging his little tail. "I am fine now!"

Canista slid right in and crouched beside her disguised cub. She licked his muzzle in greeting. "I am glad to see you again, but it is not yet safe for you to return. Shadow is very close. He wants to lead the Moon-claw pack, but they will not follow him while you live."

Storm's midnight-blue eyes sparked with fear and anger. "Perhaps we should face him and fight him!"

Canista showed her sharp white teeth in a proud smile. "Bravely said, Storm. But Shadow is too strong for you to face alone. And I am still too weak from his poisonous bite to help you. Use this puppy disguise to hide from Shadow. Go to the other world and return when you are stronger." She winced and her eyes clouded with pain.

Storm huffed out a warm glittering puppy breath. It shimmered around Canista's wounded leg in a golden mist and then sank into her gray fur. "Thank you. The pain is fading," she rumbled softly.

Suddenly, another fierce howl seemed to tear at the icy air.

"Shadow is coming! Save yourself.
Go . . ." Canista urged.

Bright gold sparks ignited in the tiny
puppy's wavy reddish-brown fur. Storm
whined as he felt the power building
within him. The golden light around
him grew brighter. And brighter . . .

Chapter
ONE

Tessa Churchill's tummy lurched with excitement as she saw all the huge trucks and trailers in front of Harpford Manor. There were lights and equipment everywhere and lots of people pushing carts and racks of costumes.

"I still can't believe that I'm going to be in *Timepiece* with Donny Jenton. I'm so nervous," Tessa said to her mom.

"That's not surprising. This is your first part in a movie," Mrs. Churchill said, giving her a hug. "Come on, let's

go and find Judith Raunds, the woman
who will be taking care of you."

Tessa nodded as she and her mom
began walking toward the main house.

She was also looking forward to
meeting the other two girls who had
parts in the movie—Tessa had been

excited to hear that they were about the same age as her. It would be great to hang out with new friends while she was here.

A woman came out of a side door and greeted them both. "Hello, Mrs. Churchill, I'm Judith. And this must be Tessa. I'm delighted to meet you." She had a light-brown ponytail and a nice round face and was wearing a blue T-shirt, jeans, and sneakers.

Mrs. Churchill shook Judith's hand. "Hello, Judith. It's nice to put a face to the voice. And thanks for being so understanding when I called to say we'd be arriving late," she said.

Judith smiled. "No problem. Delays at airports are a fact of life these days."

She turned to Tessa. "Let's go inside. Kelly and Fay arrived earlier. They're having dinner. I'll introduce you."

"Okay." Tessa smiled at Judith who seemed really nice. She felt herself starting to relax. She turned to her mom. "I'm fine. You don't have to stay with me."

"Sure? All right then, sweetie. I'll get going." Mrs. Churchill kissed her daughter on the cheek. "See you next week. And don't forget to call."

"You bet! Give my love to Dad when you get back to the yacht. Bye!" Tessa said. She waited until her mom drove off and then followed Judith into the house.

They went through a maze of

hallways until they reached a very large room. It had paneling on the walls and a high domed ceiling, which was painted with clouds and angels. Expensive-looking paintings of very serious people were hung all around.

A self-service counter with hot and cold food had been set up along one wall and there were neat rows of tables and chairs. The room buzzed with voices and laughter.

"This is where you'll have all your meals. Catering is 24/7, so you can get a hot drink or food whenever you want it," Judith explained. She led Tessa over to two girls who were sitting at a table by themselves. "These are your young costars, Kelly Lucas and Fay

Hinson. Kelly, Fay, this is Tessa
Churchill."

"Hi," Tessa said, smiling.

Fay and Kelly smiled back.

"I'll leave you all to get to know one
another. I've got a few things to do, so
I'll come back in a bit and see if you
need anything," Judith said to Tessa.

"Okay, thanks," Tessa said, smiling at the two girls as Judith moved away.

Kelly's friendly expression suddenly changed. "So you're the kid with rich parents. I bet you loved keeping everyone waiting, so you could get all the attention when you *finally* arrived!" She looked about twelve years old, two years older than Tessa, and had a thin face and short dark hair.

Tessa felt her face turning red. At her first acting school, she was bullied because she had rich parents, so now she kept quiet about it. Kelly must have listened to Judith on the phone to her mom and heard about the trip on the family yacht, which Tessa was cutting short to work on this film.

Tessa took a deep breath to calm her nerves before answering. "Let's get something straight, Kelly. Acting is all that matters to me and I just want to do my best, just like you. So leave my mom and dad out of it. Okay?" she said.

Kelly looked surprised and even a little impressed. She looked like she was going to say something else and then she shrugged. "Whatever," she said, getting up and wandering over to the service counter.

Tessa looked at Fay, hoping that the other girl might be easier to get along with. "Which acting school do you come from?" she asked her.

"Ashton School of Drama," Fay
murmured without looking up. She was
stirring her plate of pasta around with a
fork and seemed to be in a world of
her own.

Tessa tried again. "Have you seen
Donny Jenton yet?"

"No. Someone said they'd seen his
little pug dog, Lady. So he's here. But

there's tons of security around him. We'll probably only get to meet Donny when we're acting in a scene with him," Fay said gloomily. She pushed her plate away and slouched forward to rest her chin on her elbows.

Tessa felt her spirits sinking. Fay definitely didn't seem any more bothered than Kelly was about making friends with her.

A wave of loneliness rose in Tessa as she wished that she'd asked her mom to stay a little longer. But she pushed back her shoulders and resolved to make the best of it.

Tessa decided to go straight up to her room and start unpacking. She didn't feel like eating and there didn't seem to

be any point in sitting here with Fay
and Kelly.

Tessa rose to her feet. "How do I get
to our room?" she asked Fay.

Fay looked up at last. She had
freckled skin and hazel eyes and would
have been pretty if her face hadn't been
screwed into a frown. "Um . . . through
that door, up two sets of stairs, and turn
left. It's the third room you come to."

"Thanks." As Tessa went out, she
passed Kelly who was on her way back
to the table with a glass of Coke. "Too
good to sit and eat with us, are you,
Princess?" the older girl mocked.

Tessa ignored her, but she felt a lump
rising in her throat as she remembered
what it was like to be bullied. Well, she

wasn't a scared little kid anymore. She
was ten years old and had been in tons
of TV commercials and theater plays
and she was determined not to cry.

Bolting up the stairs two at a time,
Tessa found their room easily. She saw
that her suitcase had been brought up

and left on the rug. She looked around. The two beds on either side of the window had been taken. The only one left was in a gloomy alcove. There was barely room for the bed, a small bedside cabinet, and a battered-looking dresser.

"This just gets better!" Tessa grumbled, picking up her suitcase and dumping it on her bed. She opened her suitcase, grabbed a bunch of clothes at random, and opened the dresser. The door swung wide open with a loud, rusty squeak and Tessa was blinded by a dazzling bright gold flash.

"Oh!" Tessa gasped, staggering back. When she could see again, Tessa saw a tiny puppy with wavy reddish-brown fur, floppy ears, and bright midnight-blue eyes looking up at her from the bottom of the wardrobe.

"Can you help me, please?" it woofed.

Chapter
TWO

Tessa stared down at the tiny puppy in complete surprise, wondering where it had come from. The dresser door squeaking open had made it sound like the puppy had spoken! Tessa shook her head at the silly idea.

"What are you doing in there?" she said, bending over to look more closely at the puppy. "You are so cute! You look like a little spaniel."

"I have arrived here from far away. I am Storm of the Moon-claw pack. Who are you?" the puppy woofed.

Tessa's eyes widened in shock and the pile of clothes slipped from her numb fingers and crumpled to the floor. "You really c-can talk," she gasped in amazement.

The puppy nodded, looking up at her with large, intelligent blue eyes, as if waiting for her to reply to its question. Although it was tiny, it didn't seem to be very afraid of her.

"I'm . . . um . . . Tessa Churchill. I'm an actress. I'm here to make a movie."

The puppy dipped its tiny head in a formal bow. "I am honored to meet you, Tessa. I must hide. Can you help me?" he said in a gruff little bark.

"Is someone chasing you?" Tessa asked. She still couldn't quite believe that this was happening, but her curiosity was beginning to get the better of her shock.

Storm's big dewy eyes sparked with anger and fear. "Shadow, the evil lone wolf is looking for me. He has killed my father and three litter brothers and wounded my mother. He wants to lead the Moon-claw pack but the other wolves are waiting until I am strong enough to lead them."

Tessa frowned. "But how can you lead a wolf pack? You're just a pu—"

"I will show you! Please stand back," Storm interrupted in a soft bark.

He leaped out of the dresser and stood on the carpet. There was another dazzling flash of bright gold light and sparks sprayed out, floating down around Tessa and crackling where they landed.

"Oh!" she gasped as the tiny puppy vanished and in its place there stood a muscular young silver-gray wolf. Tessa nervously eyed the wolf's large sharp teeth and powerful paws that seemed much too big for his body. "Storm?"

"Yes, Tessa, it is me. Do not be afraid. I will not harm you," Storm growled gently.

Before Tessa had time to get used to the majestic sight of Storm as a young wolf, there was a final bright burst of light and he reappeared in the room as a tiny puppy with wavy rusty-colored fur and a swishy tail.

"That's an amazing disguise. No one would know that you're a wolf," Tessa said, deeply impressed.

"Shadow will know if he finds me. I need to hide now," Storm whined.

Tessa saw that he was starting to tremble all over. With his startling midnight-blue eyes, wet reddish-brown nose, and little pointed face, Storm was the most adorable thing she had ever seen.

Her heart went out to the helpless little puppy who needed a friend as much as she did.

"I'll look after you. You can sleep here with me—" she began and then stopped as she realized that pets probably wouldn't be allowed. "I could try and hide you, but I'm sharing this room with two other girls. Fay's all wrapped up in herself, so she might not notice. But I bet Kelly would love to tell on me, just to get me into trouble!" she guessed.

Storm showed his little pointed teeth in a doggy grin. "I would love to stay here with you, Tessa. I will use my

magic so that only you will be able to see and hear me."

"You can make yourself invisible? Cool! Then there's no problem. You can stay in here and Kelly and Fay won't know a thing." Tessa bent down to pick Storm up and pet his soft little head.

"Thank you, Tessa!" Storm snuggled up to her, wagging his little red-brown tail.

She was glad that her bed was in the dim alcove now. It would be much easier to cuddle up with Storm and talk to him without attracting attention from her roommates.

As Tessa put Storm down and then picked up her clothes to hang them up, the tiny puppy jumped onto her blanket. He gave a contented sigh and curled up for a nap.

Tessa smiled to herself in delight. This was better than any film and Kelly's and Fay's unfriendliness didn't matter anymore. She wouldn't be lonely now that she had this amazing magic puppy for company.

Tessa woke up early the following

morning. She could feel a warm weight tucked into the crook of her arm. Feeling her stir, Storm sat up and stretched.

"Hello, Storm. Did you sleep okay?" Tessa whispered so that the other girls couldn't hear her.

"Very well. This is a good place," Storm woofed.

The bedroom door opened and Judith popped her head in. "Rise and shine, everyone!" she said brightly. "Come down for breakfast as soon as you can, please. School lessons start in an hour."

"Okay. I'll be right there!" Tessa said.

Judith flashed a smile at her before going out and closing the door.

"It's a shame that our schools have to send us work. I can't wait until I'm older

and then I can act all day," Tessa
whispered to Storm.

Kelly jumped up, got straight out of
bed, and went to the bathroom, but
Fay sat up blinking and rubbing her
eyes sleepily.

Tessa wasn't surprised. Fay had been
writing something in a big green book

for a long time before she went to sleep. It was there on top of her night table.

"Is that your scrapbook?" Tessa asked Fay. She knew that most kids who went to acting schools kept a book of clippings and photos from their performances.

"It's my diary and it's private," Fay said, slipping the book into a drawer and slamming it shut.

"Okay. I just asked," Tessa murmured as she threw back her blanket and quickly got dressed.

Storm trotted invisibly at Tessa's heel as she came downstairs to the dining room. The delicious smells of eggs and bacon and toast floated toward them.

Tessa asked for a big breakfast and then slipped bits of bacon and egg under the table for Storm when no one was looking.

Lessons with Judith started immediately. Storm curled up for a nap on Tessa's lap. When a tiny rumbling snore rose from him, it was all Tessa could do to stifle her giggles.

It was history today and Tessa worked steadily, but she was glad when class finished for the day. "I wonder when the director will want us," she commented to Storm as she, Fay, and Kelly put away their schoolbooks.

"Duh! When he's ready," Kelly scoffed. "Or maybe you think you deserve special treatment, Princess?"

Tessa blushed. She must have spoken louder than she meant to and Kelly had heard and thought she was talking to herself. She realized that she was going to have to be a lot more careful about keeping Storm a secret.

"Stop calling me 'Princess'! I don't like it!" she snapped at Kelly.

"Okay, Your Royal Highness," Kelly crowed.

Chapter
THREE

"Fay Hinson, Kelly Lucas, Tessa Churchill to wardrobe and makeup, please!" a woman with a clipboard called out later that afternoon.

Judith Raunds showed them the way and they all set off eagerly.

"Yay! This is it. We're going to get our costumes and have our hair and makeup done," Tessa whispered to Storm as he trotted beside her.

There was a big sign that read "Wardrobe" on one of the rooms. Inside thousands of gorgeous dresses hung in neatly labeled rows and there were countless shelves and racks of hats, gloves and shoes, and wigs on stands. Assistants fetched armfuls of Victorian clothes, complete with underwear, petticoats, and black boots for the three girls.

As Tessa was helped into her costume, she noticed that her name was sewn into every item, just like a real movie star. Once the girls were dressed they went to hair and makeup. A whole hour passed before Fay, Kelly, and Tessa were finished. Tessa hardly recognized herself under the curly brown wig! She did a twirl in front of Storm so that her skirts swung out with a silken rustle.

Storm tucked his little rusty-colored tail between his legs and looked up at her with anxious midnight-blue eyes.

"What's wrong? Don't you like it?" Tessa whispered after quickly checking that everyone was busy.

"It is a very good disguise," Storm woofed. "But who is the fierce enemy you are hiding from?"

"I'm not hiding from anyone," Tessa

reassured him. "I have to wear this for the film, the same as Kelly and Fay. We're all dressed up because we're supposed to be three Victorian children who find a magic watch. We have to act in three scenes. You'll get the idea when you see us on set."

"Where is on set?" Storm barked.

"It's anywhere the day's filming is going to be. They set up lights and pieces of scenery. And the floor's marked out so you know where to stand to say your lines."

Storm frowned. "It sounds very strange."

Tessa smiled. "I expect it does if you're not used to it. Acting is really

like having the most amazing game of
pretend. It's just the best."

"I like games, too, especially with
balls and sticks," Storm yapped, looking
much happier.

"I'll see what I can do about that
later," Tessa promised.

A young man with another clipboard
appeared at the door and called for
them to follow him to the rose garden
at the back of the house.

Tessa let Judith, Kelly, and Fay walk
on ahead, so that she could talk to
Storm without anyone noticing. At first
the tiny puppy kept treading on her
long swishing skirts and almost
tumbling over his own paws.

"You'll have to walk a little farther

away or you'll get swept off your feet," Tessa told him, trying not to laugh and hurt his feelings.

Storm finally got the idea and padded behind Tessa, keeping his distance.

The rose garden was surrounded by clipped hedges. There was a pretend stone arch and a wrought-iron seat made of painted wood. Thick cables trailed across the ground and there were huge bright lights and cameras all over the place.

Tessa noticed that Fay went and stood all by herself. She was threading her fingers and looking very pale and tense. For the first time Tessa wondered if Fay's seeming unfriendliness was really just a bad attack of nerves.

A tall young man dressed in an old-fashioned dark suit and a shirt with a stiff, high collar walked through the stone arch.

"Look! That's Donny Jenton!" Tessa said excitedly.

"Wow! He's *much* better looking in real life!" Kelly gushed.

Tessa bit back a grin. Kelly was obviously too busy thinking about Donny to think up one of her usual mean comments!

A man got up from a canvas chair which had "Director" on the back and started giving Donny instructions. While they were all waiting for the scene to begin, Tessa saw a woman with a fat little dog on a leash. It had short fawn-colored fur, bulging brown eyes, and a dark muzzle, and wore a collar with "Lady" in sparkling jewels. The woman doled out doggy treats and Lady chomped them all up with a slobbering noise.

Storm licked his lips and gave a hopeful little woof.

Tessa smiled. "That must be Donny's dog. The way Lady's devouring those treats, she'll eat them all in a minute. It looks like Hollywood pooches get the star treatment, too, doesn't it?" she whispered to him. "Don't worry. You won't get left out. I'll get you a treat later."

Everyone watched in silence as Donny's scene was filmed. He had to say his lines over and over again, while the director shouted, "Keep rolling!" to the cameras.

The director seemed really strict. Tessa began to feel nervous and started fidgeting.

"Are you all right?" Storm barked worriedly.

"I'm worried about messing up my lines," Tessa whispered.

"I will help you," Storm yapped
eagerly.

"Thanks, but it's just stage fright.
Everyone gets it," Tessa said, smiling. It
was sweet of Storm to offer to help.
But what could he do? After all, he was
just a helpless little puppy.

An assistant came up to Tessa and
handed her a gold-colored pocket watch
to hold. "When he tells you to, the
director wants you to walk over to
Donny and give this to him. Okay?" she
asked with a kind smile.

Tessa nodded.

"How come *you* get to give Donny
the watch?" Kelly complained after the
assistant had left. "I've got more lines
than you. It should be me who does it!"

"Don't blame me. I'm just doing what I'm told," Tessa said, wandering away before an argument started. It hadn't taken long for Kelly to go back to her old self.

"Your laces are untied." Storm leaped forward and started snapping at Tessa's boot lace, which was trailing on the ground.

"Thanks, Storm, I could have tripped over that," Tessa said, horrified by the idea of falling in front of everyone.

She found a low wall to sit on and carefully placed the watch beside her before crossing one leg over the other to retie the boot.

To her annoyance Kelly dashed over and sat down on the wall next to her.

She really hoped Kelly wasn't going to start teasing her again. But instead Kelly smiled warmly. "Break a leg, Tessa!" she said, which was something actors often said to each other. It meant good luck for acting in the coming scene.

"Er . . . thanks," Tessa said, wondering why Kelly was being so friendly all of a sudden.

"See you on the set," Kelly said abruptly. She got up and hurried away, her long skirts swishing.

Tessa frowned, puzzled. "What was that all about?" she said to Storm.

"I do not know," Storm woofed, but he was watching Kelly closely and his midnight-blue eyes were thoughtful.

"The director's almost ready for you.

Let's move a bit closer," Judith told
Tessa. "You'll be on first."

Tessa's heart began to beat fast. It was
a good thing she was still sitting down
because her legs had turned to water.
"Oh, I need the pocket watch!" she
remembered.

She reached under her skirts and felt
along the top of the wall, where she'd
placed it. But it wasn't there.

Tessa looked all around for the watch. She checked on the other side of the wall in case it had fallen over, but there was no sign of it. "It has to be here. I only put it down a minute ago. Oh, this is awful! The director's going to be furious!" she cried in dismay.

Storm gazed fixedly at Kelly who was watching Tessa with a smug look on her face. His little muzzle wrinkled in a growl. "I have an idea where it is!"

Suddenly, Tessa felt a warm tingling sensation flowing down her spine.

Something very strange was about to happen.

Chapter
FOUR

Tessa watched in utter amazement as huge gold sparks ignited in Storm's wavy reddish-brown fur and his ears and tail crackled with electricity. Raising a little front paw he sent a burst of glittery light zooming toward Kelly.

The light divided up into glowing streamers which whizzed up and down and around and around her as if searching for something. Then, just as if someone had given them a signal, all the streamers shot toward Kelly's dress pocket and disappeared inside. No one else seemed to have noticed anything and Tessa realized that only she could see Storm's magic at work.

Tessa saw Kelly's pocket bulging and churning as if it was filled with Mexican jumping beans.

Kelly stiffened. Her eyes widened. "Ye-ow!" she yelled. Grabbing handfuls

of her skirts, she shook them wildly so that her pocket tipped open and something shiny fell out and plopped onto the grass.

"The watch!" Tessa said, realizing all at once how Kelly had distracted her before stealing it off the wall.

Storm gave a triumphant little woof and then sat down, looking pleased with himself as every last gold sparkle faded from his fur.

"Thanks, Storm. You're the best!" Tessa whispered, petting his little head after quickly checking that no one could see her doing it.

Kelly stood looking down at the watch lying on the floor as if it might jump up and bite her. As Tessa bent down to pick it up, Kelly edged away. "I wouldn't touch that if I were you. There's something weird about it!" she warned.

"Seems fine to me," Tessa said, holding the watch. "How come it was in your pocket anyway?"

"I . . . er . . . saw you drop it. And I was just coming over to give it back to you," Kelly said.

"Yeah, right," Tessa said, annoyed. "That was a really mean trick to play just so I'd get into trouble. I bet you were hoping the director would ask you to give Donny the watch instead. You're just a scene-stealer!"

"I'm not . . . I didn't—" Kelly shouted.

"Quiet on the set!" the director's annoyed voice interrupted. He glared at Tessa and Kelly. "I don't need this. Someone figure it out. Now!" he shouted.

Tessa saw Judith striding toward them with a stern look on her face. "I expected more from you two. What's going on? Out with it!" she demanded.

Kelly froze and threw Tessa a scared look. "I . . . um. It w–was . . ." she stammered.

However angry Tessa was, she wasn't a tattletale. She thought quickly. "I couldn't find the pocket watch for our scene. And I got worried that the director would be angry. Luckily Kelly found it and she was just giving it back

to me. Sorry. I didn't mean to make a scene," she apologized to Judith.

Kelly's mouth dropped open in shock. "Um . . . Tessa's . . . right. That's exactly what happened. I'm sorry for getting angry, too," she said.

Judith looked from one girl to the other. She didn't seem convinced but after a moment she nodded. "No harm done, so we won't say anything else about this. But please remember that you need to behave yourselves on the set at all times if you want to be taken seriously as actresses."

"We will," Tessa said.

"Definitely," Kelly agreed. When Judith had walked away out of earshot, she grudgingly turned to Tessa. "You're not so bad for a spoiled rich kid, Princess."

"Thanks for nothing!" Tessa murmured, barely managing to contain her anger as Kelly walked away.

The final call for her came and Tessa had just enough time to flutter her fingers in a tiny wave to Storm. Then excitement took over as Tessa prepared for her first scene with a major Hollywood star.

"And—action!"

Despite her nerves, Tessa remembered her lines perfectly. When she stood on the right mark and gave the watch to Donny he winked at her encouragingly. Time seemed to fly and then she had to pretend to be shy and run away.

"And—cut!"

"Thank you, Tessa. Good job," the director said. He turned to Kelly and Fay and waved to them to come onto the set.

Tessa sat on a chair with Storm on her lap, watching Fay and Kelly act. They were both good but Tessa had goose bumps while Fay was speaking. It was obvious to everyone that the shy girl had something special.

"She just lights up when she's acting," Tessa said, stroking Storm's silky head. "I wish I was that good."

"You are. You just don't see it in yourself," Storm woofed loyally.

"Okay, we're done for now." The director glanced toward Judith. "I'll

need all the girls back on Thursday afternoon."

Tessa felt a little disappointed. Thursday was two whole days away.

Judith smiled as she led them back to wardrobe and makeup. "Good job. This director doesn't say very much, but I could tell that he was happy with all of you."

Later that day when Tessa and Storm were alone, Tessa gave the little puppy a big hug. "And you were great today, too, Storm. I didn't know you could do magic like that! Thanks for getting the gold watch back from Kelly."

"You are welcome," Storm barked happily.

After dinner, Tessa took Storm for a walk. He rushed around, ears flapping, as he investigated the flower beds and sniffed around the trees.

Back in the big house, Tessa called her mom and dad.

They were delighted to hear all about the scene she had acted in with Donny. "And how about the other girls? Are they nice? Did you become friends with them?" Mrs. Churchill asked at the end of the conversation.

"I have made one great new friend," Tessa said, beaming at Storm.

Tessa said her good-byes and went up to her room. Storm scampered eagerly upstairs beside her.

Fay was sitting on her bed in a pool of light from her reading lamp. She wore a pair of yellow pajamas with pink teddies and had her diary open on her lap. "Where's Kelly?" she asked Tessa.

Tessa shrugged. "I don't know. Maybe she's in the living room. Judith and some other people are in there watching a movie on TV. It was great today, wasn't it? I really love acting."

Fay smiled shyly and her hazel eyes sparkled. "Me too. It wasn't half as bad as I'd expected. I was really dreading it."

"But you were really good. Everyone thought so," Tessa said, surprised. Fay had said her lines perfectly and she'd only had to do them once before the director was satisfied.

"Do you think so?" Fay asked anxiously. "I always try so hard, but I never think I'm good enough."

"My dad says that you can't do any more than your best," Tessa told her. "That's what I think of when I get stage fright."

"I'll remember that. Thanks," Fay said. She got into bed and slipped her diary into her night table before turning off the lamp. "Night. See you in the morning, Tessa."

"Night, Fay."

Storm leaped onto Tessa's bed and turned around in circles, making himself a soft nest in the blanket. As Tessa got undressed, she smiled to herself. Perhaps she might leave Harpford Manor with more than one new friend after all.

Chapter
FIVE

After class the following morning, Judith drove Fay, Kelly, and Tessa, with Storm invisibly snuggled up on her lap, into the nearest big town. "I thought we deserved a treat, and since you're not needed until tomorrow we have some spare time," she told them.

"I wonder where we're going," Fay said to Tessa as Judith looked for somewhere to park.

"We'll find out in a minute, won't we?" Kelly mocked. "How come you

and Princess are suddenly all buddy-
buddy, anyway?"

"We're not!" Tessa snapped without
thinking and then she noticed Fay's
hurt look. "I mean, we are kind of . . .
And if you don't stop calling me
'Princess' . . . !"

"Huh! Who dented your crown?"
Kelly drawled.

"Look!" Fay called hurriedly as they passed a movie theater. "Donny Jenton's latest film is showing."

"I know," Judith said, grinning. "That's where we're going."

The film was great. It was all about thieves who are trying to steal a rich prince's fortune, and had tons of special effects. Meera Brook, a gorgeous young actress, was starring with Donny. She had long dark hair and wore amazing dresses.

They all watched the movie screen, spellbound.

Storm was a bit scared of the loud noises and flashing lights at first but he soon settled down and enjoyed the movie when he realized there was no danger. "See, Storm, it's all just pretend," Tessa said soothingly.

Storm took the movie very seriously. He growled when Donny's carriage was attacked and woofed excitedly when Donny rescued Meera from a horrible bandit with a bristling beard who was slashing around with a curved sword.

"Oooh, Donny looks so hot!" Kelly said. "I wish I was Meera Brook."

After the film ended, Judith took them all for pizza. Tessa got permission to go into the superstore that was two doors down. She went straight to the pet department and bought a small bag of doggy treats and a dog bone.

Once they all got back to Harpford

Manor, Tessa found a quiet spot outside
to give Storm his treats.

"These taste good," he woofed,
licking his chops.

"Well, I don't see why Lady should
be the only pampered dog around
here!" Tessa said. "But if you eat too
many you'll soon be a little porker!"

Storm polished off the dog bone, too, and then flopped onto the grass and rolled onto his back with his tongue hanging out. Tessa smiled as she rubbed his fat rusty-colored tummy. She felt a surge of affection for the gorgeous little pup. "I wish you could stay with me forever. When I become a famous actress, you can travel everywhere with me."

Storm rolled onto his front and then stood up and shook himself. "That is not possible. One day I must return to my own world and lead the Moon-claw pack. Do you understand that, Tessa?" he asked, his midnight-blue eyes wide and serious.

Tessa nodded sadly, but she didn't

want to think about that now. She decided to change the subject instead. "Would you like to take a long walk before I call Mom and Dad?"

"My favorite thing!" Storm woofed, eagerly wagging his tail.

They went down tree-lined paths and past clipped hedges until they came to a gate leading to an open field with a river at the bottom. Colorful wild flowers swayed in the grass and there was a footpath that seemed to lead to a village in the distance.

Storm lifted his head, his little brown nose twitching. Suddenly, he shot forward like a rocket. "Rabbits!" he yapped happily.

Tessa smiled as Storm zigzagged after

the rabbits, his short, sturdy legs going
like pistons. They scattered in all
directions and shot down their rabbit
holes. Storm didn't seem to mind that
they all avoided him easily. He was
happy with snapping at disappearing
white cottontails.

After half an hour, Storm ran over to
Tessa, panting heavily, with his floppy
ears flying out behind him.

Tessa bent down to pat him. "You

look worn out. I bet you're thirsty after all that running around. Let's go back and you can have a drink in our bathroom. It'll be quieter than the kitchen and no one will notice what we're doing."

As they got closer to the main house, Tessa saw Fay sitting on a bench, reading *The Stage* newspaper in a patch of late afternoon sunlight. Tessa waved to her and Fay waved back.

Tessa and Storm went inside the house and made their way straight upstairs. As she approached their room, Tessa heard someone chuckling. "That sounds like Kelly. What's she up to?"

"I do not know," Storm yapped suspiciously.

Tessa saw that the older girl was lying on her bed on her tummy. She was reading a thick book with a familiar green cover. "That's Fay's diary! You shouldn't be reading it!" Tessa exclaimed.

Kelly looked up guiltily. "Oh, it's only you," she said.

"Put it back in the drawer right now!" Tessa demanded.

"Or what," Kelly sneered. "I've got a right to read stuff she's written about me, don't I? I know she's jealous of me because I've got more lines to say and Donny likes me better than you or Fay, I can tell."

Tessa lunged forward and tried to grab the diary, but Kelly held it out of her reach. "Stop reading it. It's private," Tessa said, kneeling on the bed.

Kelly ignored her. "Listen to this," she began, reading aloud. "It's hard to keep up with the others. I always take forever to learn my lines. Everyone else seems to know what to do, but I have to keep asking. They're all better than me at acting." She sniggered. "How funny is that?"

"Give me that diary," Tessa said through clenched teeth.

Kelly sat up. "Have the stupid thing. It's boring anyway. She hasn't written a single word about me. Catch!" she said, throwing the diary across the room.

It crashed to the floor with a thud

and landed heavily on one corner. The cover bent and twisted and some pages fell out.

"Oops!" Kelly said. "I'm out of here. See you!" She ran out and Tessa heard footsteps hurrying down the stairs.

Tessa bent down to pick up the diary. "Look at the condition of it now! Fay's going to be so upset."

"I will help you fix it," Storm offered.

Tessa felt another warm tingling feeling trickle down her spine as Storm's rusty-colored fur lit up with bright gold sparks and his floppy ears glittered with power. A fountain of golden light arched toward the book in Tessa's hands.

Tiny gold sparks like busy worker bees zizzed all over the diary, which squirmed in Tessa's hands as Storm's magic went to work.

Suddenly, Tessa heard footsteps again on the stairs. "Tessa, are you in there?" called a voice. "They've got ping-pong. Do you want to play a game?"

"Oh, no! It's Fay!" Tessa whispered desperately.

Chapter
SIX

The sparks in Storm's fur instantly
went out. Tessa looked down at the
diary. It looked worse than before. The
cover was all lumps and bumps, one
corner was badly dented, and even
more pages were hanging out.

"I did not have time to finish my
magic with Fay so close," Storm woofed
apologetically.

Tessa quickly put the diary behind
her back as Fay walked in.

"Hi. I've been looking for—" Fay
broke off, looking puzzled, and her

smile faded. "What do you have behind your back?"

Tessa gulped. She knew that Fay would be deeply upset if she found out that Kelly had been reading her private thoughts. She slowly brought her hands forward. "I . . . um . . . just came in and found this lying on the bed. I was going to put it back in your drawer, but I dropped it and the cover got a little messed up. Sorry," she finished lamely.

Fay frowned. "I *never* leave my diary on my bed."

"Maybe you forgot this time?" Tessa suggested.

Fay's face darkened. "No, I didn't. Have you been reading it?" she said in a trembling voice. "Don't try and

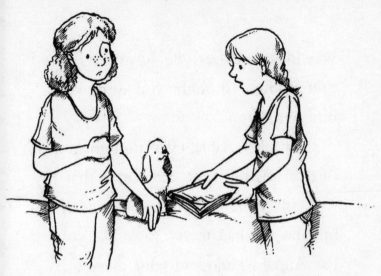

pretend you weren't. I bet you thought my scribbles were so pathetic that you kicked my poor diary all around the room and then jumped on it or something!"

"I didn't. I would never do that!" Tessa exclaimed.

"Looks like it, doesn't it?" Fay snatched her diary and then stood there hugging it to her chest and stroking it. "I thought you liked me, but you were only pretending. I thought you were different, Tessa."

Tessa felt terrible, even though none of this was her fault. She knew that Fay wouldn't believe anything she said now, but she still had to try. "I *do* like you, Fay. And I didn't read your diary. Honest. Cross my heart and hope to die!"

But Fay wasn't listening anymore. She threw herself onto her bed, buried her face in her pillow, and curled up with both arms wrapped around the diary.

Sighing heavily, Tessa trudged toward the bathroom.

Storm padded in after her and she closed the door behind him. "I am sorry. I have made things worse," he woofed sadly.

Tessa pet his silky head. "You were only trying to help. Besides, this is all Kelly's fault."

Tessa emptied a soap dish and washed it out before pouring water into it for Storm. "And just when I thought I was starting to get along with Fay," she murmured as she watched the tiny puppy lapping thirstily.

The following day it was classes again and then hours spent in costume and makeup before filming another scene with Donny. This time it was inside Harpford Manor's great hall.

It was a long scene and Tessa had a

lot of lines to say. The director was very demanding and bossed everyone around but seemed satisfied with the way things went.

When he called for a coffee break, Tessa decided that she'd go and sit with Fay to try again to make things right. She passed Kelly, who was sitting munching on a bag of chips.

"I wouldn't bother looking for Fay if I were you," Kelly said. "She's gone off somewhere by herself. I bet she's writing more stuff in her stupid diary."

"Get lost, Kelly!" Tessa said angrily, having to make a huge effort not to say something even worse. "Grrr. Why does that girl have to be so

mean?" she complained to Storm.

There wasn't enough time to go
looking for Fay, so Tessa got a cold
drink and then sat down with Storm.
"Fay probably hates me now. I bet she'll

never speak to me again," she said to
him.

"I do not think that anyone could
hate you," Storm woofed, patting her
leg with one soft little rusty paw.

"Thanks, Storm." As Tessa reached
down and took hold of the loyal pup's
paw, she felt herself starting to calm
down. An idea popped into her head.
"Why don't we walk across the field to
the village later? Maybe it will have a
store that sells diaries. I can buy Fay
a new one!"

Storm nodded. "I think Fay would
like that."

"She'll probably think I'm just trying
to make up with her because I've got a
guilty conscience," Tessa guessed. "But at

least it might make her feel a little
better."

"You have a very kind heart, Tessa,"
Storm yapped, wagging his tail.

"Try telling Fay that!" Tessa sighed.

The call came for filming to
begin again and the actors started
moving toward the set. Tessa gave Storm

a quick pat and went back to work, feeling a little better about everything.

"I was proud of you all today," Judith said to them later as they all ate dinner together. "The director was even more demanding than usual. But you just did as he asked."

Tessa was feeling really full. She'd asked for another big meal, so that she could share it with Storm. But it was difficult to slip food under the table to him, with everyone talking to her, and she'd had to eat most of it herself.

"I wish we got to see more of Donny," Kelly commented wistfully. "I'm his number-one fan, but I haven't even had a chance to ask him for his autograph."

"He's known to be a private person when he's not working," Judith said.

Fay was picking at her baked potato and salad. After only eating a little, she asked to be excused and left the table.

"Is Fay all right?" Judith asked. "She's very quiet."

"She's always like that," Kelly piped up. "She's probably just trying to seem interesting and mysterious, like Donny."

"I think she's still upset because her diary got damaged," Tessa said, giving Kelly a hard look. She was pleased to see that Kelly looked a little ashamed.

"What's that about a diary?" Judith said.

"Oh, the cover got a little bent, but

it's nothing really," Kelly said. She lowered her voice. "Some people can't take a joke."

Tessa stood up before she said something really rude. She wanted to walk over to the village. "I think I'll go and get some exercise," she said to Judith as she left the table. "But first I'll get some ham sandwiches for a snack later." *At least Storm will have some dinner*, she thought.

"My goodness. Where do you put it all?" Judith said, smiling.

"I've always had a big appetite," Tessa said hastily, moving toward the counter.

She took the sandwiches and headed outside with Storm. He scampered after her, his nose twitching at the smell of the ham sandwiches. Once they were by themselves, Tessa broke them into small pieces for him.

Storm chomped them up and then licked his chops. "Delicious!"

"Ready for an extra-long walk now? As if I need to ask!" Tessa said, grinning.

As they headed toward Harpford
Manor's main gates, they saw some film
equipment stacked up to one side
beside the path. Leaning against it were
some wooden boards painted with
scenery.

Suddenly, a short little dog with a
sparkling collar and a trailing leash shot
right through the gateway. It was Lady!

"She must have run off! Lady! Come
here," Tessa called in a friendly, gentle
way. But the pug shied away and ran
sideways.

"I will catch her," Storm yapped
helpfully, bounding forward.

Lady ran headlong toward the scenery,
brushing against it as she looked for a
hiding place in this exciting new game.

One of the big lights that sat right on the top of the stack of film equipment wobbled. It was going to fall!

Tessa looked on in horror as it began to fall toward the ground—with Storm right beneath it!

Chapter
SEVEN

"Look out!" Tessa shouted.

Storm was too focused on snapping at Lady's leash to notice the danger. Tessa realized that he wouldn't have time to use his magical powers.

Without a second thought she threw herself forward. One step, two steps. *Scoop! Scoop!* By a complete miracle she managed to grab both Storm and Lady by the scruff of their necks. With a dog in each hand, she threw herself to one side as the heavy light crashed down, missing them all by inches.

Tessa stumbled and slipped, twisting her ankle. "Oh," she gasped as a sharp pain shot through her leg.

Somehow she managed to keep ahold of the two dogs as she collapsed onto the soft grass.

"Thank you for saving me," Storm woofed, looking subdued as she set him on his feet. "You were very brave."

"I'm not really. I couldn't bear it if anything happened to you," Tessa said. She put Lady down, too, but kept a firm hold on the pug's leash. As the ache in her ankle increased, she winced.

"You are hurt. I will make you better," Storm woofed.

Just then Tessa saw a tall figure walking toward the gateway. It was Donny Jenton, completely alone and without his security guards. "There isn't time. Donny's almost here!" she hissed at Storm.

A familiar warm tingling sensation flowed down Tessa's spine, but this time there was a rush of backward movement, just as if she had pressed rewind on her DVD player.

Storm's bright eyes narrowed in concentration as he huffed out a warm puppy breath of tiny gold sparkles. The glittering mist gently swirled around Tessa's sore ankle, sank into it, and she felt the pain fade away completely. There was a sudden jerking movement and Tessa was flicked forward again. She saw that Donny was still the same distance away—no time at all had actually passed!

"Thanks, Storm. That was amazing. I'm fine now," she whispered.

"Gruff! Gruff!" Lady barked, trying to wriggle free.

Donny reached out for his dog's leash. "You're Tessa, aren't you?" he said, his white teeth gleaming as he smiled. "I saw what you just did. How can I ever thank you for saving Lady?"

"It's no big deal. It just sort of . . . happened," Tessa said, blushing.

"Well, you were very brave. Maybe a little dumb, too, to risk getting squashed

by that heavy light. I don't think your parents would approve. But don't worry, I won't tell anyone," Donny said with a twinkle in his eye.

He gave Lady a cuddle. "Bad girl. Why did you take off like that?" he scolded, wagging his finger as Lady snuffed and licked his nose.

"Maybe she wanted a long run off her leash," Tessa suggested. "She probably gets bored just sitting around and being fed treats. And I hope you don't mind me saying, but she's a little overweight."

Donny raised his eyebrows. "Really? Why hasn't anyone else told me that?"

Tessa decided not to answer.

Donny put Lady down on the floor.

"Let's get you back. From now on, you're going to get a lot *more* exercise and the doggy treats are history!" He looked at Tessa. "Thanks again, honey. Can I give you a ride back up the road to the front door? My driver's parked just down the road."

"Thanks, but I've got some shopping to do. I think I'm still going to go into the village," Tessa said.

"Well, okay. Isn't there anything I can do for you? I'd like to show my appreciation for the way you saved Lady," Donny said.

"No, I don't think . . ." Tessa paused as an idea jumped into her mind. "Well, maybe there is something . . ."

Donny listened as Tessa explained her

idea and then he grinned. "I'd be happy to. How about after filming finishes tomorrow? My driver will pick you up." He gave Tessa a quick wave as he set off with Lady puffing noisily beside him.

As Tessa had hoped, there was a bookstore in the village. She did her

shopping and then decided to return to Harpford Manor along the path that ran across the field. Storm trotted at Tessa's heel, his nose to the ground as he sniffed around. The trip had been a success and Tessa now carried a bag containing a brand-new diary, covered in shiny green plastic. It even had a strap with a heart-shaped padlock and a key to lock it with.

"I really hope this cheers Fay up— even just a little bit," she said, glancing down at Storm.

But he seemed to have run off.

"Storm? Where are you?" Tessa called.

She looked across the field, expecting to see him chasing rabbits, but there was no sign of him. Puzzled, she circled around, scanning the field more carefully, and just spotted the tip of Storm's rusty-colored tail as he dove into the bottom of some bushes.

She hurried over. "What's this hide and seek—" she began and then stopped as she realized that Storm was trembling all over. She bent down and looked through the tangled branches at him. "What's wrong?"

"Shadow has found me! He has put a spell on those dogs!" Storm whined in terror, his midnight-blue eyes wide and fearful.

"What dogs, Storm?" Tessa looked up. In the next field a man with two black-and-white sheepdogs was herding

some sheep into a pen. The dogs
were running back and forth and
snapping at the sheep's heels.

"I don't *think* those dogs are after
you. But how can I tell if they're under
a magic spell?" Tessa asked Storm.

Storm whimpered and went deeper
into the bushes. "They will have pale
cold eyes and extra-long teeth. And be
very fierce and strong."

Tessa looked hard at the sheepdogs, which were following their owner's orders closely. "They don't look like that. I think they're okay. But you've had a bad scare. Let's get back," Tessa said.

Storm squirmed toward her and she bent down and reached for the terrified puppy. As Tessa set off again with Storm in her arms, she felt his little heart fluttering against her hand. The glimpse of possible danger reminded Tessa that Storm might have to leave suddenly in order to save himself.

She felt a pang as she realized that however much she might try to prepare herself for losing Storm she would never be ready to let him go.

Chapter
EIGHT

The moment Tessa and Storm reached Harpford Manor, they went to find Fay and give her the new diary. Tessa checked the living room and the game room before she finally tracked her down in their bedroom.

Fay was reading a book. She looked up as Tessa came in and gave her a small smile.

Tessa felt encouraged. At least Fay seemed willing to talk. "Good book?" she asked hopefully.

Fay nodded. "It's fairy stories, with

really great illustrations. See? Ogres, goblins, and monsters, and there's a handsome prince who rescues a beautiful princess from a swamp monster."

"Sounds exciting," Tessa said, even though she didn't think she'd enjoy reading it herself. She went and peered over Fay's shoulder. "The prince looks a bit like Donny. Don't show it to Kelly or she'll get drool all over the page!"

Fay giggled. "Tessa. I wanted to talk to—" she began shyly.

"Okay, but me first," Tessa said quickly, thrusting the plastic bag at Fay. "I got you this. I hope you like it."

"For me?" Fay's eyes widened as she reached inside the bag and took out

the shiny new diary. "Oh, it's awesome!
And it locks, too. Look at this cute little
key."

"Yes. So no one can read your diary
now," Tessa said. "Look, about the other
evening. I know you probably still
won't believe that I didn't read—"

"But I do believe you!" Fay broke in
excitedly. "That's what I was about to
tell you just now. I came in here and

caught Kelly reading my diary earlier
and she admitted everything. She didn't
even bother lying. Anyway, I know that
you had nothing to do with what
happened."

Tessa took a second or two to let this
sink in. "Good. So . . . um . . . we can
be friends now?"

"If you still want to," Fay said, her
hazel eyes sparkling. "And thanks so
much for my new diary. I love it."

"You're welcome," Tessa said, beaming.
"And guess who I just saw on the way
to the village when I went to buy it.
Donny Jenton!"

"Really? Did he have tons of
bodyguards with him?" Fay asked.

"No. He was all by himself. He

was looking for Lady, who had escaped and run away." Tessa told Fay about running after Lady and almost getting flattened by the heavy light but she left out all mention of Storm. "Donny was so happy that Lady was safe that he offered me a reward. At first I couldn't think of anything I wanted. But then I asked if he'd take me and my friends out for a burger or something."

"You didn't!" Fay said, deeply impressed. "What did he say?"

Tessa smiled. "He was so cool. He's arranging for his car to pick us up after we finish filming tomorrow."

"Wow! That's so cool!" Fay exclaimed. "Wait until Kelly hears about this!"

"Hears about what?" Kelly demanded

from the open doorway. "As if I'd be interested in any of your pathetic plans!"

"So you don't want to hear about how Fay and me are going out for a burger with Donny tomorrow evening?" Tessa said casually.

"What? Don't make me laugh!" Kelly said. "Ugly Fay and silly, spoiled Princess going on a date with Donny? Yeah, right!"

Tessa did not show her anger. She shrugged. "Well, I guess you'll see for yourself when Donny sends his car for us."

"Yeah, right!" Kelly crowed, but she didn't look so sure of herself now. "Why would he want to take you two clowns anywhere?"

"Because Tessa saved Lady from getting squashed when some equipment almost fell on her," Fay said. "Isn't that right, Tessa?"

Tessa nodded. "Donny's *my* number-one fan now. I might get his autograph for you, if you ask me really, really nicely!" she teased Kelly and was happy

to see the older girl flush with jealousy. She turned to Fay. "Want to play a game of ping-pong?"

"You bet!" Fay cried, linking arms with Tessa. They skipped past Kelly with Storm trotting invisibly after them.

"I don't believe a word of it. You're just a big liar, Tessa Churchill!" Kelly shouted after them.

"Am I? We'll see," Tessa replied smugly.

Halfway down the stairs Tessa and Fay clapped their hands over their mouths and started to laugh. "Did you see the look on her face? You are *so* bad!" Fay whispered through her fingers.

"I couldn't help it!" Tessa answered. "I really enjoyed standing up for myself for once. Besides, Kelly won't be left out for long. I'll tell her tomorrow that she's invited to come with us!"

Tessa held up her long skirts as she emerged from wardrobe in full costume the following morning. "I can't believe that this is my last day of filming. It's gone by so fast!" she whispered to Storm.

Storm nodded, his midnight-blue eyes looking a little troubled.

"Are you looking forward to coming home with me? Mom and Dad are going to love you," Tessa said.

But Storm didn't answer. She noticed that he kept glancing nervously around as he followed Tessa down to the big old-fashioned kitchen where the scene

was being filmed. "Is something wrong?" she asked him.

"Shadow is very close now. I can feel it. He will use his magic to make any dogs nearby hunt me down," the terrified puppy barked, beginning to tremble like a leaf.

"Oh, no!" Tessa gasped, going cold all over. "Maybe it's another false alarm."

Storm shook his head. "Not this time."

Tessa racked her brains, trying to think of what to do. "I know! How about hiding in the costumes? There are thousands of them. It would be hard for any dogs to find you in there. As soon as I finish this scene, I'll come and get you."

"It is a good plan," Storm agreed. He ran off, ears and tail flying.

Somehow Tessa followed the director's instructions and remembered all of her lines. The second she was free, she ran off toward wardrobe.

As Tessa reached it, Storm shot toward her in terror, ducking into a side room. There were three dogs hard on his heels. They had pale eyes and extra-long teeth and were growling fiercely.

Tessa's heart missed a beat. Her plan hadn't worked! Storm was in terrible danger.

She rushed after the tiny puppy and fierce enemy dogs just as a dazzling flash of gold light stopped her in her tracks. When the light faded, Tessa rubbed the sparkles from her eyes to see that Storm stood there, a helpless puppy no longer, but his true magnificent wolf self. An older female wolf with a gentle face stood next to him.

Tessa realized that the moment she had been dreading was here. She was going to have to be very brave. "Go!

Save yourself, Storm!" she cried, her voice breaking.

Storm's midnight-blue eyes shone with affection, and gold dust glimmered in his thick silver-gray neck-ruff. "Be of good heart, Tessa. You have been a true friend," he said in a velvety growl.

There was a final bright gold flash and Storm and his mother began to fade before disappearing forever. The

other dogs leaped forward, but they
were too late. Their eyes and teeth
instantly returned to normal and they
left.

Tessa gulped. It had all happened so
fast. She felt stunned. "I'll never forget
you, Storm," she whispered as tears
pricked her eyes.

Tessa had just finished drying her eyes
when Fay popped her head into the
room. "I've been looking for you. It's
almost five thirty. We have to get out of
these costumes before we go and meet
Donny. I told Kelly that we're *all* going
for a burger. You should have seen her
face!"

"I bet it was priceless," Tessa said,
smiling despite herself.

As she went with Fay, Tessa felt herself beginning to get excited again at the thought of meeting up with Donny Jenton—she knew so many people who would give anything to be in her place.

But whatever the future held, Tessa knew that her secret magic puppy friend, Storm, would always be the true star of her life.

*About the Author

Sue Bentley's books for children often include animals, fairies, and wildlife. She lives in Northampton and enjoys reading, going to the movies, relaxing by her garden pond, and watching the birds feeding their babies on the lawn. At school she was always getting yelled at for daydreaming or staring out of the window— but she now realizes that she was storing up ideas for when she became a writer. She has met and owned many cats and dogs, and each one has brought a special kind of magic to her life.

Read all of the other books
in the Magic Puppy series!